# Living in
# Italy

## Ruth Thomson

### Photography by David Hampton

## SEA-TO-SEA
*Mankato Collingwood London*

This edition first published in 2007 by
Sea-to-Sea Publications
1980 Lookout Drive
North Mankato
Minnesota 56003

Copyright © Sea-to-Sea Publications 2007

Printed in China

Library of Congress Cataloging-in-Publication Data
Thomson, Ruth, 1949-
    Living in Italy  /  by Ruth Thomson.
      p. cm. -- (Living in--)
    Includes index.
    ISBN-13: 978-1-59771-043-5
    1.  Italy--Juvenile literature. 2.  Italy--Social life and customs--Juvenile literature.  I.
Title: Italy. II. Title. III. Series.

DG451.T56 2006
945--dc22

                                                                                  2005057110

9 8 7 6 5 4 3 2

Published by arrangement with the Watts Publishing Group Ltd, London

Published by arrangement with the Watts Publishing Group Ltd, London

Series editor: Ruth Thomson
Series designer: Edward Kinsey

With thanks to Kathryn Britton

# Contents

# This is Italy

Italy is one of the easiest countries in the world to recognize on a map. Shaped like a high-heeled boot, it juts into the Mediterranean Sea, in southern Europe. Its pointed toe appears ready to kick Sicily toward Sardinia—two islands which are also part of Italy.

**△Mountainous Alps**
The Alps in the north form a border that separates Italy from Switzerland, France, Austria, and Slovenia.

**▷The Po River**
Italy's longest river winds through the plain. It provides water for irrigating crops, such as rice, fruit, sunflowers, and vegetables.

**△The Po Valley**
A large, low-lying plain, called the Po Valley, lies at the foothills of the Alps. This is the most densely populated and heavily industrialized area in Italy.

Fact Box

**Population** 57.9 million
**Capital** Rome
**Official language** Italian
**Main religion** Roman Catholic
**Highest mountain** Mont Blanc (15,770 ft/4,807 m)
**Longest river** Po
**Biggest cities** Milan, Naples, Turin, Palermo, Genoa, Bologna
**Currency** Euro

4

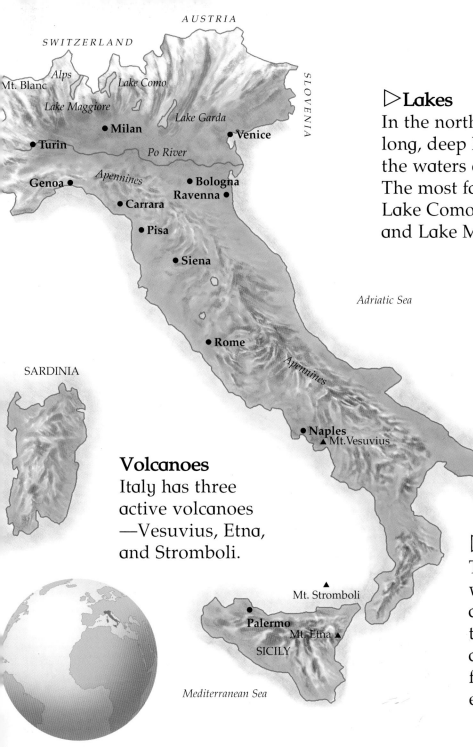

AUSTRIA

SWITZERLAND

Mt. Blanc

Alps

Lake Como

SLOVENIA

Lake Maggiore

Lake Garda

● Milan

● Venice

● Turin

Po River

Apennines

Genoa ●

● Bologna

Ravenna ●

● Carrara

● Pisa

● Siena

Adriatic Sea

SARDINIA

● Rome

Apennines

● Naples
▲ Mt. Vesuvius

## Volcanoes

Italy has three
active volcanoes
—Vesuvius, Etna,
and Stromboli.

▲
Mt. Stromboli

● Palermo

Mt. Etna ▲

SICILY

Mediterranean Sea

## ▷Lakes

In the north, there are
long, deep lakes, fed by
the waters of the Alps.
The most famous are
Lake Como, Lake Garda,
and Lake Maggiore.

## ◁The Apennines

The Apennine
Mountains form a
620-mile (1,000-km)
backbone down the
length of Italy. In
places such as
Carrara there are
marble quarries.

## ▷The south

The south is far drier,
wilder, less populated,
and less visited than
the rest of Italy. It is
an area that suffers
from occasional
earthquakes.

# Rome—the capital

Rome is not only the busy capital of modern Italy, but it was once the powerful center of the ancient Roman Empire. Ruins of ancient Rome—walls, baths, temples, a racetrack, carved columns, roads, and burial vaults, called catacombs—can be seen all over the city.

### △The Roman Forum
The Forum was the heart of ancient Rome. People came here to shop, worship in its temples, go to court, or do business.

### △The Trevi Fountain
Legend has it that visitors who want to come back to Rome must throw a coin over their left shoulder into this fountain.

### ◁The Colosseum
In ancient Roman times, this massive amphitheater held 50,000 spectators. They watched gory fights between gladiators, slaves, prisoners, and wild animals.

### ◁ Saint Peter's Basilica
Saint Peter's, the biggest church in the world, is in Vatican City. Its huge dome rises above the site where Saint Peter is thought to be buried.

### ▷ Swiss Guards
Vatican City has about 100 Swiss Guards. Their costumes date back to when they were founded in 1506.

### ▽ Castel Sant'Angelo
Originally constructed as a tomb for the Roman Emperor Hadrian, this drum-shaped building was converted into a fortress for the popes. A passageway links it to Vatican City.

# Vatican City
The world's smallest country, Vatican City, lies within Rome. It is the headquarters of the Roman Catholic Church, led by the Pope. It has its own passports, coinage, postage stamps, radio station, car license plates, and an army of Swiss guards to protect it.

# Famous sights

Italy itself is like a museum. Everywhere you go, there is something of interest to see. There are historic old towns, ruined castles, splendid palaces, magnificent cathedrals and churches, and hundreds of ancient Roman sites.

## Natural wonders

There are also national parks in the mountains, where rare animals, such as the brown bear and wolf, are protected.

◁ **The Leaning Tower of Pisa**
Built on sandy soil, this bell tower started leaning during its construction in the 13th century. Over the centuries, it has tilted farther. To make it safe, earth has been removed from under part of its foundations.

△ **The Galleria in Milan**
This glass-domed arcade of cafes, stores, and offices was built nearly 150 years ago. It was one of the first buildings in Europe to be constructed of steel and glass.

## △ The Grand Canal, Venice
Venice is a unique city, built on more than 100 islands, with canals instead of roads. The largest is the Grand Canal, lined with elegant palaces. Tourists can travel along it in unusual-shaped boats, called gondolas.

*A poster advertising an exhibition of mosaics*

### ◁ Ravenna mosaics
Ravenna's churches are decorated with splendid mosaics. Some date back as far as A.D. 600.

### ▽ Designer outlets
In big Italian cities, there are streets of elegant boutiques selling designer clothes, shoes, and jewelry.

# Living in cities

More than three-quarters of Italians live in towns or cities. Many towns have a historic center with narrow streets and old buildings. The heart of the town is a square *(piazza)* with a grand palace or church. Some piazzas also have a fountain or the statue of a famous local person.

AREA
PEDONALE
URBANA

△**Car-free area**
Cars are banned from most historic centers.

▷**A piazza**
Piazzas are places to meet and chat.

*A statue of Garibaldi*

PIAZZA
GIUSEPPE GARIBALDI
(1807 – 1882)

A
GARIBALDI
RAVENNA
1892

◁ **Street names**
Streets are often named after Italian heroes. In 1860, Garibaldi led 1,000 volunteers to free Naples and Sicily from French rule.

△ **The suburbs**
Suburbs have grown up outside larger towns.

▽ **Tourist guides**
Most places produce guides for their many visitors.

▷ **Living in apartments**
Most people live in apartments. They do not have gardens so they often decorate their balconies with flowers and hang their laundry out of the windows.

# Around town

Days in towns have a particular rhythm. The streets are busy all morning with workers and shoppers. By early afternoon, they are deserted as stores and businesses close for several hours. Lunch is the biggest meal of the day for most Italians.

△**Travel in town**
Traffic is heavy in most big towns. Special lanes for buses help them move quickly. Many people used mopeds for short journeys.

△**Town signs**
Illustrated signs point the way to important and useful places.

▷**Restaurant meals**
Meals are divided into courses. Cold meats or seafood are followed by pasta. The main dish is meat or fish. Vegetables are served separately. Meals end with coffee and dessert.

△**Police (*polizia*)**
Traffic police
make sure the
traffic keeps
flowing at busy
intersections.

◁**The *passegiata***
In the late afternoon
and evening, people
come to shop,
people-watch, and
meet friends.
Italians call this
evening stroll the
*passegiata*.

▷**Having a snack**
Stopping for a pastry
and coffee, a sorbet,
or an ice-cream cone
is an essential part of
the *passegiata*.

## Summer days in town
In the hottest months, people often take
a rest in the afternoon. When the day
begins to cool, the stores reopen.
The town center bustles as people
of all ages come out again.

▷**Opening times**
This sign shows winter
opening hours. During
the summer, some shops
do not reopen until 4 or
5 p.m. and stay open until
8 or 9 o'clock at night.

ORARIO di APERTURA

dalle  MATTINO  alle

dalle  POMERIGGIO  alle

GIORNO DI CHIUSURA
INFRASETTIMANALE    DOMENICA

# Living in the country

Far fewer people now live in the country than in the past. Farming has become increasingly large-scale and mechanized, so not as many farm workers are needed to do the work.

△ **Churches**
Every village has a church, often with a tall bell tower that can be seen for miles around.

▷ **Villages**
Many villages perch on a hill. Some date back to medieval times and had walls built around them for protection.

△ **Villagers**
Villages are increasingly populated by the elderly. Young people who cannot find work in the country move to towns and cities. They often return to their home village on weekends and for holidays or vacations.

## Regional farming

Each region, however, still grows its traditional crops. Farmers whose cows graze on Alpine pastures produce butter and cheese. Those in the Po Valley grow wheat and rice or tend fruit orchards. Farther south, farmers have olive groves or vineyards.

◁**Sunflowers**
Sunflowers are an important crop. They are grown for their seeds, which are pressed into oil for cooking.

▷**Vineyards**
Wine is one of Italy's major exports. Rows of vines cover the sunny hillsides of areas with rich, well drained soil.

◁**Mechanized farming**
Farms in the Po Valley use big machines to sow and harvest their crops.

Zucchini flowers like these are eaten as well as the vegetable itself.

# Shopping

There are fewer supermarkets and large department stores in Italy than in many other Western countries. Instead, there is a huge variety of small, specialist stores. Most towns also have a daily or weekly market.

△**Markets**
Many markets sell clothes and household goods, as well as food.

△**Food stands**
Food stands open only in the mornings, so people can buy fresh fruit and vegetables for lunch, as well as supper.

▷**A traditional grocery store**
A grocery store, like this one, sells hams, hard cheeses, preserved and roasted meats, olive oil and vinegar, jam, honey, cookies, and other everyday foods.

The baker *(la panetteria)*

The fishmonger *(la pescheria)*

The butcher *(la macelleria)*

A toyshop *(giocattoli)*

## △Specialist stores

People buy fresh food from separate stores. There are also individual stores selling hardware, paper and pens, baby clothes, or toys.

## ▷News stand

Outdoor news stands sell train schedules and postcards as well as newspapers and magazines.

**△ Road signs**
Highways (*autostrada*) are signposted in green. Places of interest are signposted in brown.

# On the move

Car ownership in Italy is one of the highest in the world, with one car for every two people. Air pollution has become a big problem in major cities. Some have tried introducing electric cars and car-free days in the city center.

Highways crisscross the country connecting big cities and towns.

*Open*

*Closed*

**▽ Service stations**
Service stations are often situated on the outskirts of towns and villages, where there is plenty of space.

**◁ Tunnels**
Because the country is so mountainous, many road tunnels have been cut through hillsides. Long bridges called viaducts span the valleys on concrete stilts.

△ **The metro**
Both Rome and Milan
have a subway system,
called the metro. The cost
of a ticket is the same, no
matter how long the
journey is.

## The railroad network

Italy has a wide network of railroads.
Rapid Eurocity trains run between the
major cities in Italy and Europe. Fast
trains stop at main towns. Slow, local
trains stop at every tiny village station.

△ **Trains**
Italian trains have
a reputation for
always leaving and
arriving on time.

*Train tickets*

# Family life

Family life is important in Italy. Many Italians live close to their families or, if not, visit as often as possible. Family get-togethers and meals are part of their everyday life.

△Family size
Italians are having fewer children than any other European country. The population is expected to fall in the next ten years.

▷Young and old
It is not uncommon for elderly people to live with their children and grandchildren.

▽Watching TV
Almost all Italian families own a television. Soap operas, variety shows, and sports are the most popular programs.

## ▷Grandparents

Almost half of all women work, so grandparents often help with looking after children.

## ▽Family meals

On weekends, relatives may get together to have a big meal that lasts for several hours.

## Children at home

Many Italian children enjoy following sports, especially soccer, playing with Gameboys and Playstations, swopping cards, listening to the latest music, reading comic books, and watching DVDs.

21

# Time to eat

Italians love good food. Each region has its own distinct dishes, using fresh, locally produced ingredients.

Fresh fish is eaten all along the coast. In the north, people often eat dishes made with beef, rice, potatoes, or corn meal (*polenta*) made from corn.

▷ **Pasta**

Pasta is made from wheat. There are more than 200 different shapes.

*Spaghetti   Mafaldine*

*Penne*            *Conchiglie*

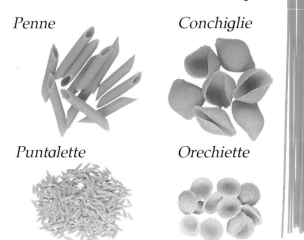

*Puntalette*        *Orechiette*

◁ **Breakfast**

Children eat cereal, a piece of fruit, or some sweet bread. Many adults have coffee and a pastry in a cafe.

▷ **Pizza**

Pizza was created in Naples. It is cooked in a wood-burning oven.

## ▷Spaghetti

Spaghetti is often eaten with tomato sauce.

## ▽Italian specialties

Many regional food products, such as these, are exported, as well as being sold in Italy.

*Olives*

*Parma ham*

*Balsamic vinegar*

*Pesto— a pasta sauce made from basil*

*Salami— cured meat*

## Other cooking styles

In central Italy, people cook with olive oil and eat more pasta, beans, and pork specialties, such as ham and salami. In the south, many dishes are based on vegetables and seafood. In Sicily, food is spiced with chilies. Sicilian cakes and pastries are very sweet and rich.

*Panettone—sweet Christmas bread*

*Pandoro— soft cake*

*Panforte —fruitcake*

*Almond pastries*

*Amaretti— almond cookies*

*Nutty chocolate*

# School time

Children go to primary school for five years. There are two kinds. Part-time schools have classes six days a week from 8.30 a.m. until 2.30 p.m. (plus two afternoons). At these schools, children do homework every day. Full-time schools run from 8.30 a.m. until 5 p.m. every weekday. Children have homework only on weekends.

*School-bus stop*

▷**Getting ready**
At primary school, children wear an overall, called a *grembule*. They take only the books they need for each day and a mid-morning snack, (*la merenda*).

▽**Starting school**
Children start school at the age of six. Those aged between three and five can go to a free full-time nursery school.

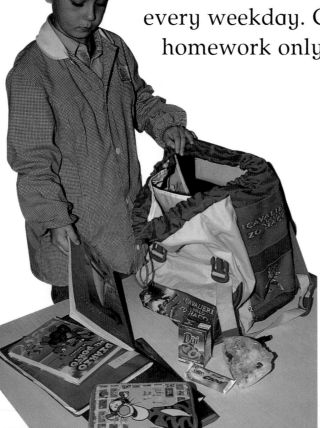

24

## Secondary schools

At the age of 11, children move to a middle school for three years. Then they choose a secondary school with an emphasis on either classics (Latin, Greek, history, and philosophy), science, languages, or technical subjects.

*Pen with built-in ink eraser*

*Grammar book*

*Homework diary*

*Storywriting book*

*Maths book*

◁ **Lessons**

The main emphasis in primary school is on learning to read and write in Italian. Some children may also start learning English.

**25**

# Having fun

Italian social life mainly takes place in town squares and streets, especially in warm weather. Friends meet in cafes and restaurants. Children often stay out late for meals with their families.

## Spectator sports

Watching soccer, motor racing, and cycle races are Italian national passions.

△ **Looking good**
Young Italians are very fashion-conscious. They like to wear designer-label clothes.

*There are lots of soccer magazines.*

△▷ **Soccer**
The Italian soccer league has four main divisions. Series A, the top division, has 18 teams, including AC Milan, Inter Milan, and Juventus. They all have their own uniforms and plenty of merchandise for fans to collect.

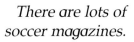

*Windsurfing in Sardinia*

## Vacations

Most Italians take their vacations in August, when the weather is too hot and stifling to stay in the cities. Businesses, restaurants, and stores in towns close down. Families head for the sea, the mountains, or a lake. In winter, many Italians go skiing.

◁**On the lakes**
Steamers zigzag up the lakes to places of interest. There are mountain trails for walkers to follow and bathing places for swimmers.

△**At the seaside**
Beaches are crowded with foreign tourists, as well as Italians. Some beaches are private and provide umbrellas and beach chairs, which people pay to use.

# Religion

A majority of Italians are Roman Catholic, although fewer and fewer people go to church every Sunday. People still celebrate Christmas and Easter Week, however, and important Christian festivals with religious events.

△ **Priests**

Priests are in charge of the churches. Some still wear long black robes, but others wear modern clothes and even have cell phones.

▷ **All Saints' Day**

On November 1st, All Saints' Day, people take flowers to cemeteries to remember their dead relatives.

△ **Holy figures**

Holy figures, such as the Virgin and Child or a saint, are often painted on old house walls. Sometimes, the figures are carved and stand in niches.

# Celebrations

Many places celebrate their local saint's day by carrying his or her statue in a procession around the town.

## Costumed festivals

Some towns stage costumed contests each year, with jousting, crossbow, flag-throwing, or horse races.

### ◁ Carnival

In Venice there is a carnival in the ten days up to Lent. People wearing costumes and masks, like these, take over the main square. The festival ends with a masked ball.

### ▷ The Palio in Siena

The Palio is a horserace held twice a year. After a parade of costumed supporters, riders from different districts of the city race bareback around the Campo (the main square) three times.

COMUNE DI SIENA

PALIO

DEL 2 LUGLIO 1994

FESTIVITÀ DI MARIA SANTISSIMA IN PROVENZANO

SINDACO RENDE NOTO: CHE IL 2 LUGLIO p.v. VERRÀ EF. ATA NEL "CAMPO", LA TRADIZIONALE CORSA DEL PALIO, ALE SI SVOLGERÀ SECONDO IL PROGRAMMA SEGUENTE:

Comparse delle Contrade e le Rappresentanze del Comune si riunir ore 16,20 in Piazza del Duomo (Cortile Palazzo del Governo) e anno per le Vie del Capitano, di S. Pietro e del Casato. Alle ore Corteo Storico, al suono della campana maggiore, farà l'ingresso mpo". Precederanno il Vessillifero del Comune con i musici di Pal Portainsegne delle Città, delle Potesterie, delle Terre e dei Castelli ti l'antico Stato Senese, comprese Rappresentanze dei Comuni di M rittima e di Montalcino. Farà seguito il Capitano del Popolo presentanti dei Terzieri di Siena lle Masse. Seguiranno le sentanze dello Studio Senese, del trato della Mercanzia e porazioni delle Arti, nonché il P reca il Masgalano con la rta e, successivamente, le Compars rade partecipanti alla c

ISTRICE - 2. BRUCO TERA - 4. O
NICCHIO - 6. AQU DIMONTO

*A costumed supporter in the pre-Palio parade*

# Going further

## Look for Italian food

Have a look in a supermarket to see what food it sells from Italy. How many different sorts of pasta can you find? What sauces can you find to go with them? What Italian cheeses are there?

Make a list of the foods. Notice whether the labels give the region the foods have come from. Find these regions on a map of Italy.

## Make a city guide

Find out more about one of the major cities that tourists visit, such as Venice, Rome, Florence, or Siena.

Make a tourist brochure, describing the city sights, using a piece of paper folded into three. Draw some pictures or glue in photographs cut out from color magazines or vacation brochures. Write short captions about each sight.

## Design a carnival mask

People wear all sorts of colorful or glittering masks to the Venice Carnival. Design your own Carnival mask. It could cover either the whole face or just the eyes. You may like to add a fancy hat, too.

## Websites

www.yahooligans.com/Around_the_world/countries/Italy

www.initaly.com

www.enchantedlearning.com/europe/italy

www.cybersleuth-kids.com (click on geography, then type Italy into the "search" box)

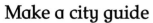

# Glossary

**Arcade**  A covered passageway with stores on both sides.

**Border**  The boundary that divides one country from another.

**Earthquake**  A shaking of the Earth, caused by movements of vast plates of rock in the Earth's crust. The most violent earthquakes happen near where the edges of the plates meet.

**Exports**  Goods that are sold by one country to another.

**Industrialized**  Having a large number of industries.

**Irrigation**  System of watering using channels and ditches.

**Mechanized**  Work done using machines.

**Medieval**  From the Middle Ages (the period between the 5th and the 15th centuries).

**Merchandise**  Goods produced that are linked with a "name," such as a famous soccer team.

**Mosaic**  Picture or pattern made by fitting together small pieces of marble, glass, or ceramic.

**Pasture**  Grassland where animals feed.

**Plain**  An area of flat land.

**Population**  The number of people living in a place.

**Quarry**  A place where rock, stone, or slate is cut from an open hillside.

**Suburb**  A district on the edge of a city where people live.

**Temple**  A place of worship.

**Vineyards**  Fields planted with grape vines.

**Volcano**  A cone-shaped mountain lying over a chamber of red-hot, molten rock, called magma. Sometimes pressure from hot gases causes a volcano to erupt.

# Index

Page numbers in *italics* refer to entries in the fact box, on the map, or in the glossary.